To Piper, for showing me how fun NOW can be

Tundra Books, an imprint of Penguin Random House Canada Young Readers,
a Penguin Random House Company

Library and Archives Canada Cataloguing in Publication
Perry, Gina, 1976–, author, illustrator
    Now? Not yet! / Gina Perry.
Issued in print and electronic formats.
ISBN 978-1-101-91952-1 (hardcover).—ISBN 978-1-101-91953-8 (EPUB)
    I. Title.
PZ7.1.P47No 2019   j813'.6   C2018-903154-9
                                           C2018-903155-7

Published simultaneously in the United States of America by Tundra Books
of Northern New York, an imprint of Penguin Random House Canada Young
Readers, a Penguin Random House Company

Library of Congress Control Number: 2018951987

Edited by Samantha Swenson
Designed by Five Seventeen and Sarah Nwabuike
The artwork in this book was created with gouache and Photoshop.
The text was set in Omnes.

Printed and bound in China

www.penguinrandomhouse.ca

1 2 3 4 5   23 22 21 20 19

Penguin
Random House
TUNDRA BOOKS

NOW?
NOT YET!

Gina Perry

tundra

"Can we go swimming now?" said Peanut.
"Not yet," said Moe. "Let's hike!"

"Now?" said Peanut.

"Not yet," said Moe. "I think I see an owl!"

"Now?" said Peanut.

"Not yet," said Moe. "It's snack time!"

"Now?" said Peanut.

"Not yet," said Moe. "I think we are lost."

"Ow. Now?" said Peanut.

"Not yet," said Moe. "Oh Peanut!"

"Now?" said Peanut.

"Not yet," said Moe. "It's time to make camp."

"Now?"

"Now?"

"Now?"

"Now?" said Peanut.

"Not yet," said Moe. "We need to set up up the tent."

"Now!" said Peanut.

"Not yet!" said Moe. "Our bags aren't unpacked, our campfire isn't ready and where are the tent poles?"

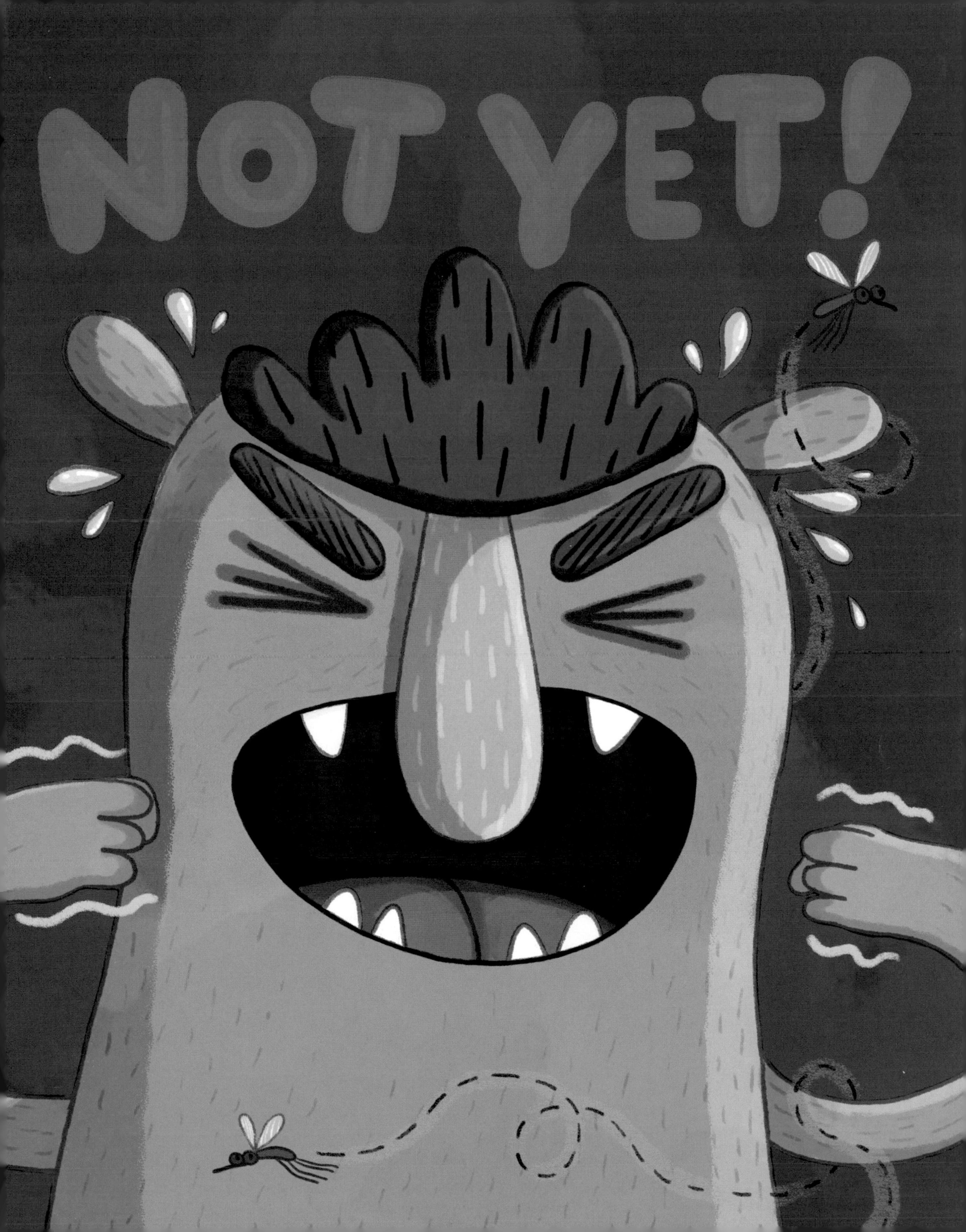
NOT YET!

"Now our tent is up."

"Now our bags are unpacked."

"Now our campfire is ready."

"Now . . . I miss Moe," said Peanut.

"Now we are dry."

"Now we are cozy."

"Now we are warm."

"Now we are happy," said Moe.

"Now is it time for bed?" said Peanut.

"Not yet," said Moe.